I found two aspects of this composition most interesting: the music and the esoteric symbolism of the cards. Musically speaking the dialogue between the guitar and magnetic tape is extremely inspiring: an excellent composition in all respects.

**Ennio Morricone**

© All rights reserved
**Gangemi Editore spa**
Piazza San Pantaleo 4, Roma
www.gangemieditore.it

No part of this publication may be stored in a retrieval system or reproduced in any form or by any means, including photocopying, without the necessary permission.

ISBN 978-88-492-2053-7

# Tarot cards
## meditation and music

*by* Bruno Battisti D'Amario

GANGEMI EDITORE

We all know that the 22 Trumps (or Major Arcana) of the playing cards known as "Tarot Cards" are considered to be like an ancient book of divination and wisdom, a " book that talks" and encourages thought and meditation.

The colours and position of the figures and objects in the cards represent an exquisite and highly symbolic ensemble: just "looking" at them sparks and fires one's imagination while their study reveals a world of analogical knowledge.

Tarot Cards can help man in his imaginal introspection by providing the iconic instruments he needs during his difficult and demanding journey through life.

As a musician and composer I've always considered music as an important, fundamental tool to help me understand myself; I've come to believe that combining the symbolic force of the "Tarot Cards" with the music with which they are intimately connected – in other words inspired by the mystery of the cards themselves – can truly help us undertake an inner journey as "fascinating as it is gratifying and fulfilling".

Mine was certainly a positive but also "frightening" experience: I found myself in front of a mirror broken into a thousand pieces, each piece reflecting a different image of me.

*Bruno Battisti D'Amario*

## What people have said about *Bruno Battisti D'Amario*

My profession often depends on the individual talent of professionals provided by organisers. As composers we try to protect ourselves by leaving as little as possible to chance, composing for people who we know will always give us quality performances.
Bruno Battisti D'Amario is one of the very few artists for whom I'd do anything just to work with him. His very perceptive interpretation is always artistically and professionally outstanding, so much so that he often leaves me, my directors, conductors, and even his own colleagues, speechless and full of admiration. For all these reasons and despite my very long career, I know very few like him. I'm always scared when I think that, for whatever reason, he might not be able to work on one of the films for which I'm composing.

*Ennio Morricone*

What people have said about *Bruno Battisti D'Amario*

… I've worked with Prof. Bruno Battisti D'Amario on many occasions and I've always been able to appreciate his technical expertise, his eager and supple musicality and beauty of sound. He's a wonderful, talented person.

*Nino Rota*

… The guitarist Bruno Battista D'Amario and I worked together during several recitals at the Contemporary Festival of Venice; his talents as a soloist, outstanding musicality and first-rate instrumental technique make him an excellent musician and player.

*Severino Gazzelloni*

What people have said about *Bruno Battisti D'Amario*

I've had the pleasure of working with Bruno
Battisti D'Amario many times and each time I've
been able to appreciate his outstanding gifts as
a unique musician and human being.
He has always excelled whether playing alone
or in an orchestra, revealing his exceptional
talents, technical skills and great musical
sensibility and sentiments.
I am certain that D'Amario is one of the few
contemporary musicians who can truly
demonstrate what it means to play a guitar.

*Bruno Nicolai*
Composer, conductor
Director of the Musical Publishing House "Edipan"

|  | I<br>THE MAGICIAN,<br>THE MAN,<br>THE INITIATE |  |
|---:|:---:|:---|
| II THE HIGH PRIESTESS | | III THE EMPRESS |
| IV THE EMPEROR | | V THE POPE |
|  | VI THE LOVERS |  |
| IX THE HERMIT | VII THE CHARIOT | VIII JUSTICE |
| XV THE DEVIL | XIII DEATH | XI STRENGTH |
| XVI THE TOWER | XIV TEMPERANCE | X THE WHEEL OF FORTUNE |
| 0 THE FOOL | XVII THE STARS | XII THE HANGED MAN |
| XIX THE SUN | XVIII THE MOON | XX JUDGEMENT |
|  | XXI<br>THE WORLD |  |

# Layout of the composition

## The composition is divided into seven parts:

### Part One

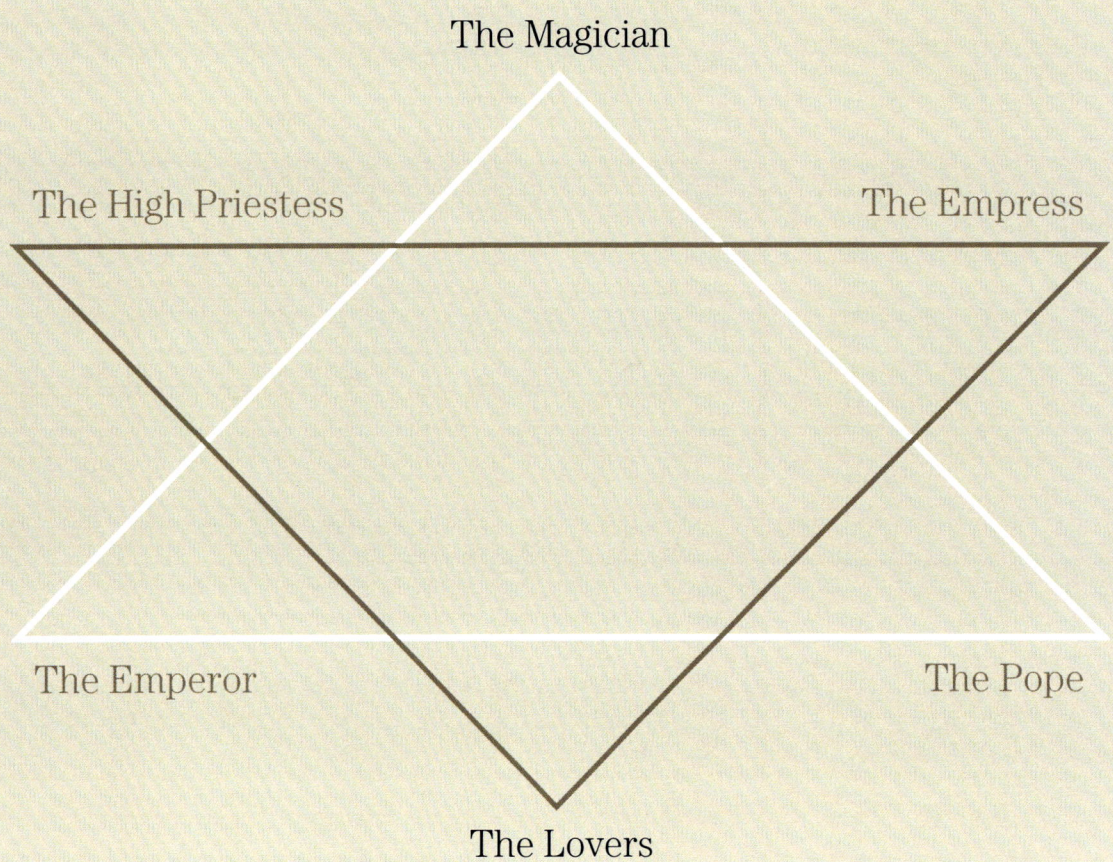

After The Lovers the next 15 tarot cards are divided into five groups (each with three Trumps) which will be considered as follows: given the energies of the first and second card (the first being mainly MASCULINE and the second mainly FEMININE) an attempt will be made to unite them and – "rectifying" – find the right relationship in order to create a new and different energy symbolised by the third card (BALANCING).

|  | Masculine energy | Feminine energy | Balancing |
|---|---|---|---|
| part 2 | IX THE HERMIT | VII THE CHARIOT | VIII JUSTICE |
| part 3 | XV THE DEVIL | XIII DEATH | XI STRENGTH |
| part 4 | XVI THE TOWER | XIV TEMPERANCE | X THE WHEEL OF FORTUNE |
| part 5 | 0 THE FOOL | XVII THE STARS | XII THE HANGED MAN |
| part 6 | XIX THE SUN | XVIII THE MOON | XX JUDGEMENT |

Part Seven involves only the n. 21 Trump, The World, and represents a synthesis of the journey that started with The Magician.

| part 7 | XXI THE WORLD |
|---|---|

*In my composition I have maintained the original numbering of the cards but not their position; this is because I believe that Tarot Cards – all Tarot Cards – represent a universe in which the cards are interchangeable and therefore can be placed in different positions depending on the character and needs of the user.*

I wrote this music for guitar and magnetic tape: the former symbolises man, his inner travails and intuitions; the magnetic tape represents his external environment, everything that surrounds and influences an individual. It also embodies the inner resonances he is unaware of.

The composition lasts approximately 64 minutes.

The performance can vary as follows:
- **Complete performance**
- **Performance of Part 1**
  (The Magician – The High Priestess – The Empress – The Emperor – The Pope – The Lovers)

- **Performance of Part 2**
  (The Hermit – The Chariot – Justice) plus, *ad libitum*, Part 7 (The World)
- **Performance of Part 3**
  (The Devil – Death – Strength) plus, *ad libitum*, Part 7 (The World)
- **Performance of Part 4**
  (The Tower – Temperance – The Wheel) plus, *ad libitum*, Part 7 (The World)
- **Performance of Part 5**
  (The Fool – The Stars – The Hanged Man) plus, *ad libitum*, Part 7 (The World)
- **Performance of Part 6**
  (The Sun – The Moon – Judgement) plus, *ad libitum*, Part 7 (The World)
- **Performance of Part 7**
  (The World)
- **Performance of the *Balancing Cards***
  (The third card of Parts 2, 3, 4, 5 and 6).
  The first four form a Suite associated with a sort of tonal dictation. By adopting an ideal approach, Justice is expressed as a Prelude, Strength as an Allemande, The Wheel as a Passacaglia and The Hanged Man as a Gavotte. Justice is expressed as a fugato

The Complete Performance has been played with the following instruments and tuning indicated below:

1. Classical Guitar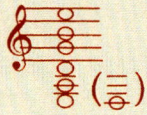

2. Classical Guitar

3. Electric Guitar

4. Baroque Guitar

*I'd like to emphasise how in nearly all the Tarot Cards – according to the precise role I have assigned them - the electric guitar evokes what is associated with chance and instinctivity.*

Before illustrating the 22 Trumps one by one, I'd like to provide a detailed explanation of part one since it inspired, instigated and steered the rest of the composition.
Tarot card n. 1 represents the Magician, the Magus, or simply a Man who voluntarily and consciously starts an introspective journey.
His first task is to analyse himself to try and identify and then separate his own basic energies traditionally symbolised by air, water, earth and fire. The latter are represented by the next four cards:
The High Priestess, The Empress, the Emperor and The Pope. Later on I will explain how the remaining 17 Trumps will always be in some ways linked to these four basic characters.

(1) *unspecified length but shorter than normal tuning.*

| | | |
|---|---|---|
| THE HIGH PRIESTESS | Water<br>*Air* | Passive feminine energy |
| THE EMPRESS | Heart<br>*Fire* | Active feminine energy |
| THE EMPEROR | Fire<br>*Earth* | Active masculine energy |
| THE POPE | Air<br>*Water* | Passive masculine energy |

Once this introspective, investigative stage is over, The Magician will review and proportionally and gradually merge the four energies, trying to create new and different states of awareness. Card n. 6 (The Lovers) closes this phase; we could call the card an "apprenticeship", an initial moment of insight; it is the moment when we become aware of the Love that allows us to understand others, to achieve the Tolerance we so desperately need to continue our journey.

When asked how he composed such beautiful and formally perfect music, Mozart replied it was the easiest thing in the world "… just couple notes that love each other …"

I'll now give a short explanation of how I have interpreted the symbolism of the 22 Major Arcana and how I have musically translated the way in which the cards are connected. I will also provide some short but necessary technical details (on the back of the cards).
*The notes I have chosen for each card represent a symbology strictly inspired by numbers. In some esoteric schools the number THREE is associated with the first level of "physical" awareness while the number FIVE, primarily femminine, is linked to soul awareness (this is why there are five notes in the scale of The High Priestess and The Empress). The number SEVEN embodies the sequence of notes of The Emperor and The Pope and represents the attainment of a third level of consciousness called "mental" awareness. The NINE notes (3 x 3) associated with The Hermit, The Chariot and Justice indicate a higher level of awareness compared to the previous two.*

# The twenty-two Major Arcana

*Part I* **cards from 1 to 6**

# the Magician

We've already mentioned that Man is made of with a random and jumbled set of component elements (Air, Earth, Fire and Water): his first task is to become aware of them and then reorganise them (*Ordo ab Chao*, Order from Chaos).
We can call these four elements "energies", two of which, Water and Earth, are mainly feminine, and the other two, Fire and Air, mainly masculine.
Like a modern amplifier, Man is gifted with an "input" and "output" system through which he can receive or transmit these energies.

*So I pick up my guitar and begin to sing a nostalgic song.*
*The tune of The Magician slowly twirls around me, my senses are blurred… what's happening?*
*I'm slowly sinking down inside myself, it's dark, darker and darker.*
*I begin to hear other sounds which are not, however, those of my guitar…*

*The music played with this card is intended to portray what happens when Man becomes immersed in his own indistinct inner self (symbolised by the "chaotic" sounds of the tape): he begins to notice the faint melismata of The High Priestess, the indistinct sounds of The Empress, the "harmonies" of The Emperor and the rhythmic impulses of The Pope.*
*The Magician tunes in to these sounds, surrendering to the musical crescendo which will carry him towards a final explosion, a sort of big-bang marking the beginning of his real journey.*
*Man is now alone, sustained only by the mysterious language of meaningful ancient symbols of wisdom, beauty and strength. This is the beginning of his search to discover the inner incommunicable secret that should inspire him to achieve the Great Task.*

# the High Priestess

This card marks the beginning of the analysis The Magician must carry out to separate and distinguish between his inner energies. The High Priestess is the raw material Man needs to understand he can achieve a certain expertise without which everything would be in vain. I believe the card symbolises the power that presides over what we call fantasy and imagination, an energy that is certainly very powerful, but absolutely sterile if left to its own devices.
To increase and direct this energy we must always be able to logically control it.
Echoes are created between the sounds of the guitar and those of the tape; they symbolise The Magician's attempt to tune into the inner resonances of The High Priestess – an attempt that will succeed at the end of the piece.

The composition of The High Priestess is based on a series of five sounds with intervals of minor second, major second, minor third and major third.
Intervals are the distance (expressed in pitch) between two notes.
"Minor" (-) intervals have been considered feminine and "major" (+) intervals masculine, while "perfect" (P) intervals (which we will come across later) symbolically create a balance between the two polarities.
For those unfamiliar with music, I'd like to point out that the sign for flat (b), based on the keyboard of the piano, moves the note back by one white or black key.

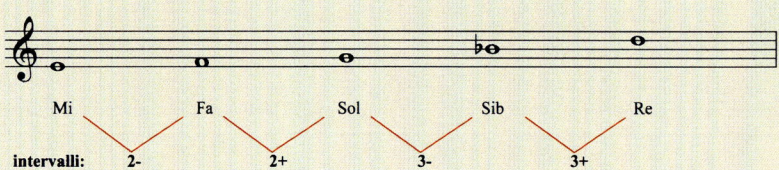

The series begins with a minor interval (feminine)
The minus sign (-) stands for minor (feminine)
The plus sign (+) stands for major (masculine)

the mpress

The Magician now has to become aware of a very dangerous force, in some ways akin to the disruptive wrath of water; the negative side of this energy explodes in Man as anger, aggressiveness, violence and intense passion.
I think we've all had a fit of rage or an uncontrolled reaction which has surprised and even slightly frightened us: why weren't we able to stop ourselves? How far will we let ourselves "go"?
It's crucial that we recognise these "waters" if we are to placate and then channel them between robust banks: only then will we be able to use them constructively.
At the end of the piece the *five* strokes regularly cadenced by the guitar, followed by another five from the tape, indicate that The Magician has been able to exercise an orderly and balanced control over this energy.

*Like the previous card there are five sounds for The Empress but with greater intervals (minor seventh, minor sixth, major sixth and major seventh). The difference between the passive energy of The High Priestess and the active energy of The Empress is expressed in music; in the first case by notes that are closer together (2° and 3° intervals) and in the second by more distant notes (6° and 7° intervals). Note that this scale also starts with a minor interval (feminine). For those unfamiliar with music, the # sign (sharp) based on the keyboard of the piano, moves the note forward by one white or black key.*

*In this piece the guitar basically acts as a percussion instrument and the musician can choose how to improvise.*

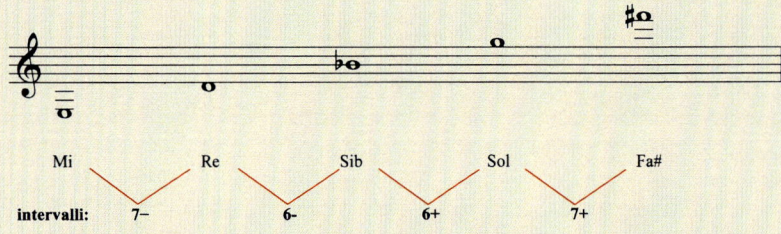

The series begins with a minor interval (feminine)
The minus sign (-) stands for minor (feminine)
The plus sign (+) stands for major (masculine)

# the Emperor

He is the sovereign of our bodily kingdom, the continually active living matter that tangibly tries to discover in the outside world the realm of what is "constant", i.e., linked to physical nature. He is strongly opposed to The High Priestess who instead searches for the realm of the "volatile", i.e., associated with our emotions (feelings, sensations, fears, fantasies, etc.).

The Magician's task is primarily to find and maintain a "correct and perfect" balance between what is *constant* and what is *volatile*: although closely interlinked, these two aspects often merge in variable, casual, rather than calculated proportions. Unlike the music of the two previous tarot cards, here it represents movement and has a very distinct marching rhythm.

Most of the next cards can be traced back to The Emperor or The Pope to which we have given a mainly masculine "character". They will be expressed by primarily rhythmic compositions, while those linked to The High Priestess or The Empress (mainly feminine) will be random ascending compositions.

*The musical series of The Emperor is based on seven sounds separated by a major second, major third, minor second and minor third with the addition of two perfect fourths. The intervals of the first five sounds of this series are the same (but with different pitches and a different arrangement) as The High Priestess. Note that the close 2° and 3° intervals are also present here, but in this case (reversing the masculine and feminine aspect of The High Priestess) they symbolize an active, masculine energy.*

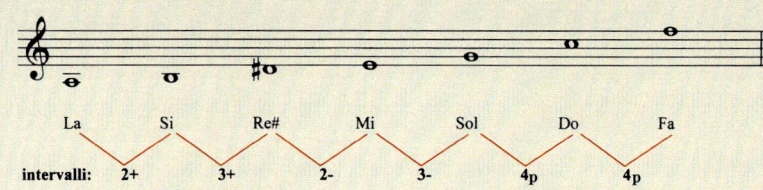

The series begins with a major interval (masculine)
The minus sign (-) stands for minor (feminine)
The plus sign (+) stand for major (masculine)
The **p** stands for "perfect" (balancing).

# the Pope

This energy is also represented using rhythmic strokes, but rather than being "projected" outwards it sinks into Man's inner being, contrary to what happens in The Emperor, and becomes palpable when the music is played.

The Pope's resolve and determination meets and merges with a multitude of inner voices with which we must start to dialogue: Faith will be the language used to communicate and the technique that of prayer, the recitation of "mantra" and rhythmic breathing.

Only when one we understand the energy of this card are we able to enter into contact with several different devotional truths.

The cadences of the beginning and end of the piece are the same as the ones in The Emperor; they indicate the vigilant, conscious attitude we have to adopt towards the inner voices that may be false or even traps (superstition or exasperated religious integralism).

*The seven sound series of this card is arranged at intervals of major seventh, minor seventh, major sixth and minor sixth with the addition of a perfect fourth and a perfect octave. We all know that music uses seven notes, so the eighth is nothing but the repetition of the first which in turn is the beginning of a new scale (1 c, 2 d, 3 e, 4 f, 5 g, 6 a, 7 b, 8 c, 9 d, 10 e, etc.).*
*Going up an octave is necessary to give added impulse and project us towards a new phase. The intervals of the first five sounds of this series are the same as The Empress (but with different pitches and a different arrangement). Note that the distant 6° and 7° intervals are also present here, but in this case (reversing the active and feminine aspect of The Empress) they symbolize a passive, masculine energy.*

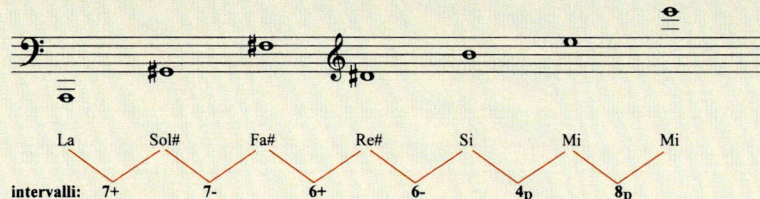

The series begins with a major interval (masculine)
The minus sign (-) stands for minor (feminine)
The plus sign (+) stands for major (masculine)
The **p** stands for "perfect" (balancing).

# the Lovers

With this card (in other decks also known as "the enamoured" or "the lover") The Magician achieves his first moment of balance and inner peace which would already allow him to live "in harmony".
Now he has to decide whether to continue his journey by being pro-active (i.e., making a conscious decision), or be satisfied with the results achieved so far and interrupt his journey.
Having reached the first level of Love and partially attained Tolerance, the fact he feels connected to his "neighbour" can be very rewarding, but also not enough.
At this point, a *Knight* "without blemish and without fear" would certainly decide to continue his journey by dynamising The Lovers.
To indicate that a first level of balance has been achieved between the masculine and feminine energies of the previous four cards, the rhythm of the guitar will be regular but less marked, and the randomness of the musical base of the magnetic tape will be less forceful.

*The series of six sounds of this Trump is created by "choosing" the third note from each of the four sets of previous notes to indicate an initial moment of merger between the four main energies, adding at the end of the series an interval of a perfect fourth ("balancing" note) and another interval of a major second (a link with the masculine energies of the next card). The (natural) sign ♮ is used to cancel a flat or a sharp from a previous note.*

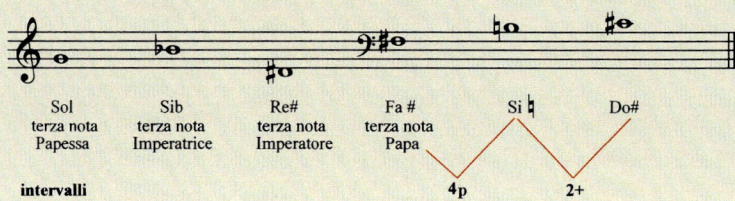

*Part II* **cards from 7 to 9**

# the Hermit

This Trump marks the beginning of a new phase which we could call "refinement".
The awareness of The Lovers has allowed Man to live a harmonious and balanced "everyday life". He now knows himself a little better and is able to choose the journey he feels most comfortable with, in other words one or all or none of the possibilities proposed by the Tarot Cards.
This is when he must look inside himself and become aware of his "inner silence".
To understand The Hermit you have to know his "key-symbol": the lantern in his right hand that must always remain lit.
This constantly vigilant "Light of reason" will not allow the next card (The Chariot) to tragically keel over; instead it will indicate a well-defined path based exclusively on the achieved level of awareness (cutting one's coat according to one's cloth!).
A note will sound during the whole piece symbolising the continuous presence of the Light. Several bundles of sounds are superimposed on this note; at first they will be slightly dissonant but at the end of the piece they will be combined in a liberating and reassuring major chord (consonant).

*The musical series is now made up of nine notes; the first four come from the sequence of sounds associated with The Emperor, the other five from the musical series of The Pope (union of active and passive masculine energies). Compared to the matrix, the nine notes of this series are inverted by an augmented semitone (indicating achievement of a greater level of awareness), except for B which remains natural: this note musically and ideally links The Hermit to the previous and next card. The base of the magnetic tape is the same as the one for The Pope except it's played in reverse.*

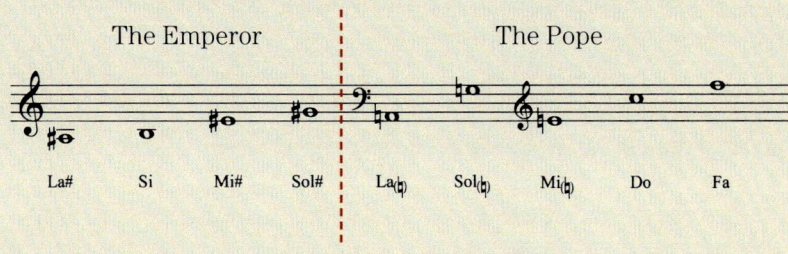

# the Chariot

Enlightened by The Hermit, The Magician must now trigger his inner Emperor whose throne, once so static, has begun to move; gradually acquiring speed, power and rhythm… it is turning into a Chariot. Change is taking place, but we must not forget that this is a particularly dangerous phase: if the Trump is not driven properly and is not balanced by the quiet wisdom of the previous card, it could crush anything under its weight and this hasty and unenlightened human Justice might even kill innocent people. It's time to take on important responsibilities: we have to know how to govern The Chariot and stop the two horses (symbol of duality) from taking separate, uncoordinated routes.
Duality exists in nature (high and low, male and female, life and death, etc.) and is often represented by a white and black chequerboard: the Chariot has to follow the straight line between the two colours.

The musical series, again with nine sounds, is the same as the one for The Hermit but a semitone lower, summarising the pitches already present in The Emperor and The Pope. The indistinct and chaotic sounds of The Empress are now well arranged and regulated by a constant rhythm recalling the music of The Emperor.
To dynamise The Chariot we will have to unite and balance active feminine energy (The Empress) with active masculine energy (The Emperor).
In this piece the guitar provides percussion and rhythm.

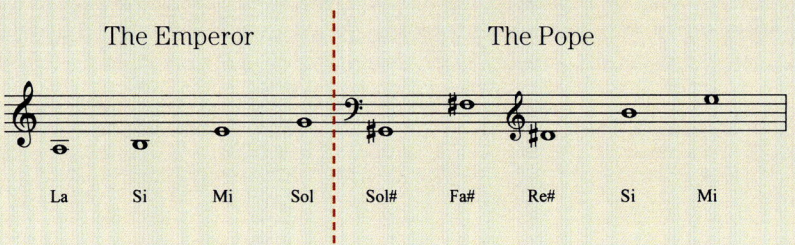

# Justice

Justice ends the first of the five triptychs in which the third card represents energy emanating from the perfect, proportioned coupling of the two previous Tarot Cards.
If we manage to combine the soul beauty of The Hermit with the (physical) force of The Chariot then we will be able to achieve the inner Justice that will allow us to exercise the necessary balance throughout our everyday life.
Trump VIII represents a higher degree of awareness and it would be unwise to try and penetrate the next Tarots without its knowledge.
All the "Third Cards – Balancing" have been ideally placed in a "pseudo-tonal" Suite. In other words although the music in the Suite is experimental it is clearly inspired by the classics. It is a composition in the composition insofar as it can be performed separately from the other Tarots and yet maintains its own musical and symbolic logic.

*The musical series is the same as the one used for The Hermit but shifted by an augmented semitone (except for the two final notes which are shifted by **two** augmented semitones: a desire to rise further!).*
*Only in the magnetic tape of the Suite (Justice is a prelude to the Suite) do we realise that there are sounds coming from another two guitars: these represent the inner voices of the previous cards which, once so indistinct, now dialogue clearly and individually with the main instrument.*

*Part III* **cards from 10 to 12**

# the Devil

This is the symbol of one of the most powerful energies in nature, of the "vortex" that can disrupt the order of things: this card embodies all the most destabilising aspects of the four elements. It is the force of egoism whose negativity tends to take possession of other people's souls; it is the fire of instinct that can destroy everything; it is the "beast" within us.

This energy exists and we don't have the power to eliminate it.

However, once understood and tamed it can be decisive in our material life; if we can conquer our fear of Death (which we will deal with in the next Tarot) we will be able to control it.

We need to imprison this card in deep, dark dungeons, and understand that as an enemy it can become – like the Genie in Aladdin's lamp – a very valuable servant. The seven deadly sins are the Devil's field of action, but those who have achieved Justice can use it to change these seven negativities into seven positivities.

At this point in the journey The Magician has to realise he was born to free himself from the tyranny of his basest instincts.

*The force of the Devil is musically expressed by a very quick rhythm with obvious reference to the music of The Emperor (active masculine energy).*
*It's also possible to hear the beat note of The Hermit; however in this case it is superimposed on the inner voices that convey negativity and is very different in nature to those of The Pope. The music is like an orgiastic dance performed in the bowels of the earth in the middle of terrifying fires and murky vapours; the music makes you realise how the energy of a "Sabbath" or a "witches' night" can blur the edges of your mind and lead to unconsciousness.*

# Death

All religions and esoteric schools consider death and resurrection as a fundamental step in the process of identification with a Superior Being. Death frees the energies needed to create new realities. Symbolically experiencing death while alive and conquering our fear of death is a technique that can lead to a different level of consciousness, very similar to rebirth. This card conveys awareness of the continuity of life. A wise man experiences this all the time, and each resurrection provides a new level of awareness. Courage and humility are the strengths needed to let parts of us die and yet continue to ask questions, especially when we think we have progressed and acquired certain truths!
The power of this Trump is so important and fascinating it can balance and turn the disruptive energy of The Devil into something positive: this balance will allow us to achieve true Strength.

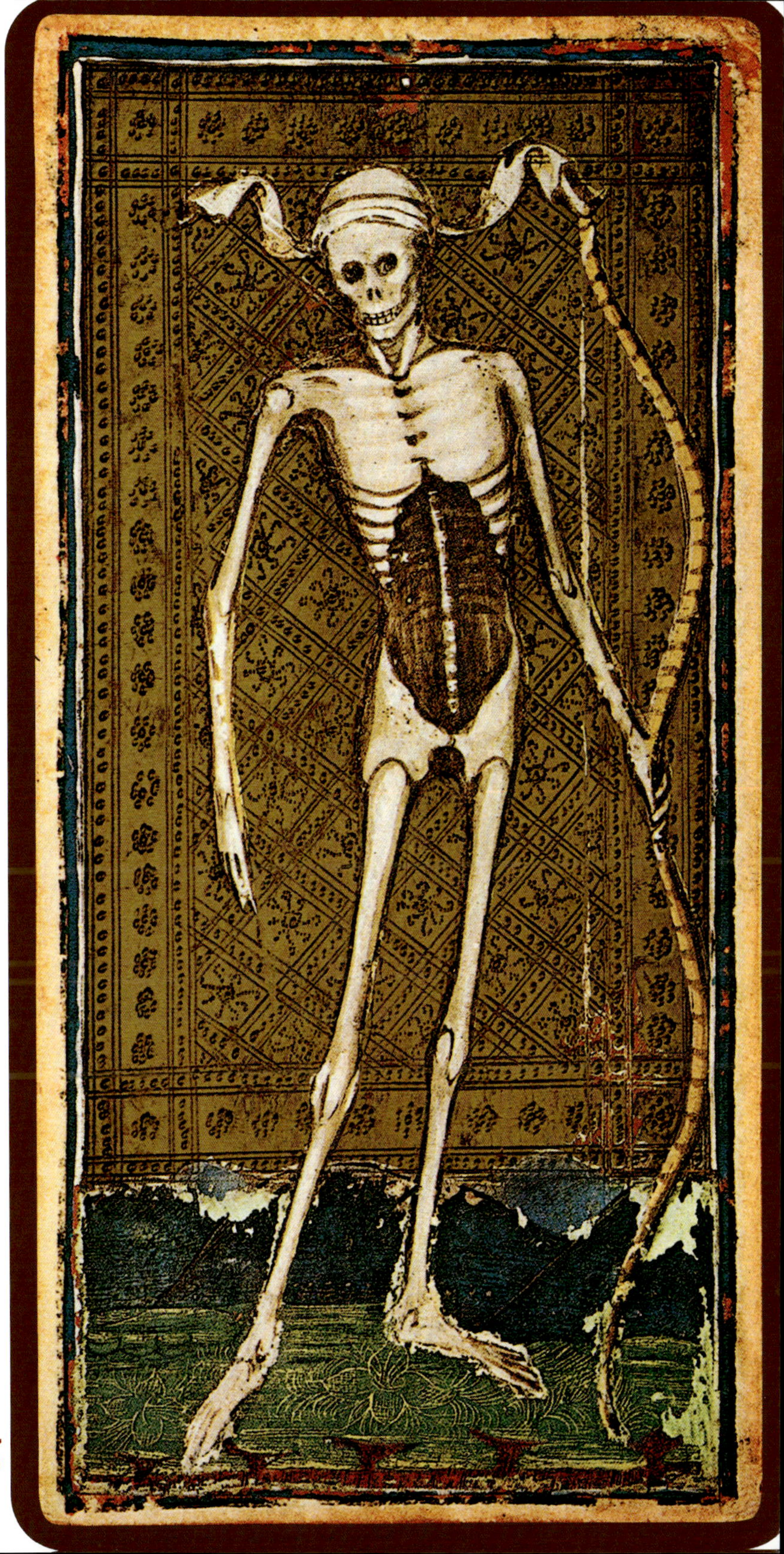

Paradoxically, the intention of the composition is to emphasise the "breath" and "vitality" of Death.

A rhythmic breath can clearly be heard – two inspirations and two expirations; superimposed on this rhythm are echoes of the music of The High Priestess, The Empress, The Emperor and The Pope. This is almost an attempt to give the four fundamental energies a synchronised and univocal rhythm.

The performer should improvise based on the rhythmic and percussion music in The Empress (active feminine energy), dialoguing with the echo of the march of The Emperor (active masculine energy), the five faint rhythmic percussions of The Pope (passive masculine energy) and the soft melismata of The High Priestess (passive feminine energy).

# Strength

Once The Magician has tamed the overpowering and devastating energy of The Devil and experienced initiation and rebirth after his journey in the realm of Death he can explore the deep, dark prisons of his basest and most uncontrollable instincts thanks to the balancing influence of this new Trump; he will be able to focus on building the Temple to Virtue "for the good of Humanity and the glory of God" and can now add "Strength" of spirit to the "Beauty" of the soul he achieved with Justice. This third part of the composition shows why all life force (even the negativity of The Devil) should be turned into positive energy, like the Alchemist who never tires of trying to turn lead into gold. This new strength is not only physical, it is also expressed in the music by notes which if represented graphically would create specific geometric figures. The square, the circle, the triangle, etc. are considered by all esoteric traditions as universal symbols of Wisdom.

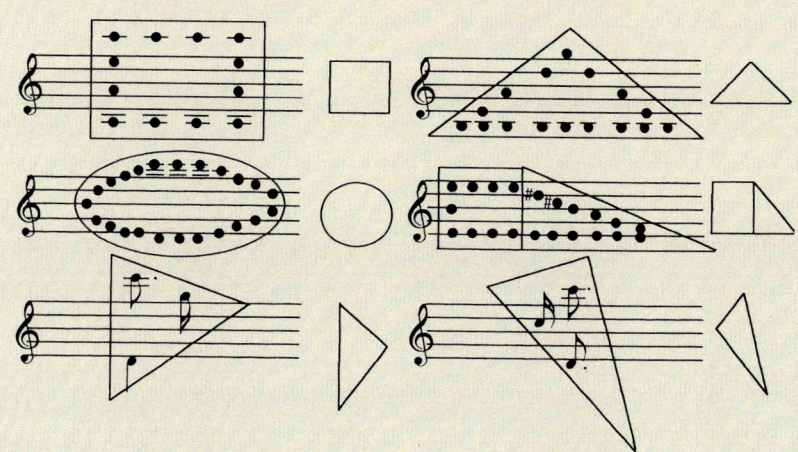

guitar

magnetic tape

guitar

magnetic tape

*Part IV* **cards from 13 to 15**

# the ower

Although the energy of The Tower is similar to that of The Devil, we have to consider it even more negative. It is the Tower Of Babel, man's negative, unbridled ambition to achieve all his goals, including truth, by ignoring any moral concept, systematically being aggressive and despotically exploiting others. It is the absurd, presumptuous desire to complete the parts of the Temple which should remain unfinished, Icarus' foolish impudence to fly close to the sun.
Three infamous lords rule over The Tower: *ignorance* that tramples the teachings of the three previous cards, disseminating errors, *fanaticism* that turns the Temple into a confined space prey to the most pernicious bigotry and superstition, and *unbridled ambition* that lets unrestrained and wanton egoism run free.
We cannot eliminate this energy (in nature nothing is created or destroyed) but we can control it like we did the Devil and if we sensibly combine it with the next Trump we will be able to reuse it.
*The three "evil lords" can be turned into three "lights".*

*The music emphasises the negative traits of The Tower with a pseudo-jazz piece (played on an electric guitar) which evolves into a series of variations and improvisations, based on the tune of The Emperor (active masculine energy) dialoguing with the percussion tunes of The Empress (active feminine energy). A fast rhythm accompanies simple ascending musical movements interrupted and slowed down, in the low register, by short descending scales. This emphasises how every creative project based on this card is fatally destined to collapse and fail. Like the tune for The Devil, here the music is like an orgiastic dance characterised by forceful rhythmic movements.*
*I remember that I assigned a rather expressive and instinctive role to the electric guitar.*

# Temperance

The symbolism of this card is very clear: the liquid in the two vases (in some decks one is silver and the other gold) is repeatedly poured from one to the other in an ongoing search for a new balance thanks to this non-stop exchange of masculine and feminine, active and passive, physical, spiritual and soul energies.

We've seen how The Tower, if left unbridled, can "burn down" or demolish every creative project: only the "humidifying" power of Temperance is able to curb these destabilising impulses.

To esoterically die means freeing oneself so as to be able to benefit from a better life where the liquid of Temperance (also called The Fountain of Youth) can forever regenerate us and in turn allow us to participate in eternal life.

When we are able to measure and "acquire" the liquid of Temperance required to control the fire of The Tower, we create the new "circular" and "continuous" balancing energy expressed by the next card: The Wheel of Fortune.

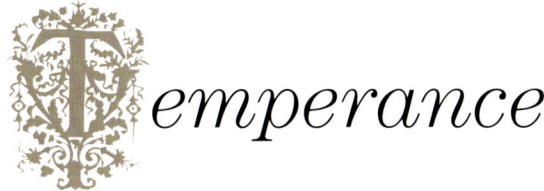

*The sound bundles repeated throughout the piece represent the continuous pouring of the vital and vivifying liquid of Temperance. It's also easy to recognise the tunes of The Lovers and Justice, "balancing" cards required to create "equality". There are also obvious references to the tune of The High Priestess indicating the chiefly feminine character of Temperance.*
*These tunes are joined by a series of small groups of notes which repropose the casual percussion sounds of The Emperor which have now turned into specific, organised pitches (improvisation is no longer haphazard but inspired by a cognisant conscience).*
*The peaceful pace of the music leads us to a quiet, soothing place conducive to meditation.*

# the Wheel of Fortune

After demolishing the obstacle of The Tower using the dynamising power of Temperance, The Magician is now able to achieve the greater awareness of the Wheel of Fortune. This card should allow us to project outwards the inner balance we achieved through Justice. In some decks this card has two concentric and seemingly static and unidirectional circles which I interpret as circles spinning furiously either clockwise (the energy of The Tower) or anticlockwise (the energy of Temperance). One of the two circles symbolises the positive energies of the spiritual growth of The Magician and encourages personal development while the other represents all the negative aspects that lead to destruction and delirium. In the centre and above the Wheel there's a static image, a Sphinx before whom Man has to present himself to govern the maelstrom of the two forces. We know that in many esoteric traditions movement inside a sacred space always has to be in the same direction (clockwise or anticlockwise, circular or square). The Magician has moved beyond this level and reached the hub of the wheel, he "walks" at his leisure in any direction. Like a real Magician or Teacher he is able to perceive a timeless and spaceless dimension.

*This is the third piece of the "Suite of the balancing cards" musically expressed by a phrase which, like a classical Passacaglia, is cyclically repeated in the same way and then reversed (retrograde) indicating the two directions of the concentric circles in the Wheel. The tune has the same notes of the Temperance (which in turn reproduces The High Priestess) and The Tower (associated with The Emperor).*

*Part V* **cards from 16 to 18**

*the* Fool

Starting with this Trump, the next group of three cards indicates a rather special journey that can lead to a different awareness. It is meant for all those who have a natural and instinctive link with higher worlds (for examples true Artists).
If the task of The Magician is to divinise matter, the task of The Fool is to "materialise" the divine inspirations he receives all the time.
His unassuming and shabby appearance should not deceive us because it undoubtedly masks a mysterious relationship with higher realities (associated with a certain type of foolishness).
The Fool starts from the infinite and arrives at the finite; his knowledge is beyond human comprehension. I have to remind myself to seek for Truth above all where appearances would seem to suggest it doesn't exist.
To appreciate this card we have to truly understand and practice Humility: a proud man who boasts of his own wisdom doesn't realise he will never achieve the same level of understanding as The Fool whose characteristic number is "zero", in other words the awareness of being all or nothing, of being able to say to someone or be told "*checkmate*".

*The composition associated with this eccentric character is nothing but a continuous series of "crescendo" which could either lead to the complete loss of awareness (madness), or just as easily generate a resolutive positive spark.*
*This is musically symbolised by the initial tune of The Magician which from this moment on and until the end of the journey will - more or less clearly - always be present.*
*Superimposed on a frenetic rhythm, the electric guitar (initially so instinctive and improvised) begins to become aware of itself: very gradually the rhythmic pace of the music dissolves and the reassuring song of The Magician emerges loud and clear.*
*It's as if at this stage of the journey "instinctivity" turns into "reason".*

# the Stars

The Fool's ability to perceive the Harmony of the Celestial Spheres using his innate inner antenna would be completely useless if The Stars didn't want to communicate and express themselves through Man.
We travel from East to West, from North to South, and even beyond our own physical limits to try and capture the messages received from other dimensions.
I don't think men are alone: on a dark night we shouldn't forget to turn our eyes to the heavens and look at the majesty and brilliance of the Stars. Awareness of this Arcana will allow us to once and for all overturn the ostensible incoherence of The Fool and reveal the path leading to the "different" consciousness symbolised by the next card (The Hanged Man).
What does our ego do when we sleep? Are dreams the echo of a higher world which we try to explore? Travelling with our soul outside ourselves when we're awake (The Fool) and controlling our physical body when we sleep (The Stars) shows we have acquired considerable skills.

*The same magical and dreamy atmosphere at the end of the previous card is also present in The Stars. When immersed in a multitude of "harmonic" sounds at close intervals, sounds that create ethereal and fascinating vibrations, we can hear the faint tune of The Magician, the same one we heard in The Fool: Man is increasingly aware of his own importance. Several short variations recall the melismata of The High Priestess and The Lovers. Towards the end of the piece the tune is "harmonised" - in other words played as "chords" - as if to penetrate the Harmony of the spheres.*

# the Hanged Man

The uncomfortable and painful position of The Hanged Man should not mislead us. His visible physical weakness means he has acquired remarkable spiritual strength, allowing him to live and work just by using his mind rather than through movement.
The reciprocal interpenetration of The Fool and The Stars has allowed The Magician to distance himself from all material things.
Once spirituality has been enhanced by actively giving up our physical and soul nature, then "Grace" will come from The Stars.
This awareness comes from feminine (or lunar) initiation and this is the journey the mystic must make.
We should explain what "distancing" means: it is a technique that is very difficult to implement. The danger lies in becoming excessively egocentric and cold towards others. Exactly the opposite of The Hanged Man who (as shown in the tarot card designed by Oswald Wirth) is able to scatter silver and gold coins on the floor even if he is in this "awkward" position.
This card perhaps provides the greatest moment of exaltation of transcendent religious knowledge which only a few noble souls actually achieve (St. Francis?).

*The position of The Hanged Man allows for only two options: to symmetrically swing like a pendulum between The Fool and The Stars or live the stillness of a central point. The melodic tune of The Magician, in this case performed reversed (retrograde) like the reality of The Hanged Man, is superimposed on a continuous, undulating rhythm.*

*Part VI* **cards from 19 to 21**

# the Sun

Unlike The Hanged Man, the Sun can move backwards and forwards because it is not in a state of absolute immobility. And yet paradoxically its fixed position triggers "perpetual motion", the cycle of night and day and the circulation of air and water on the earth's surface. The heat and light from the sun give birth to vegetation as it does to everything else conducive to life.

*The trials and tribulations of our life on earth are there to "teach" us: when we pass these tests we are compensated with final initiation.*
We should act so that the true light of The Sun can embrace us with its warmth and strength, only then will we find the lost word and reforge the broken key.

*To achieve full understanding of this crucial Trump, The Magician will have to carefully study the sun's activity during the night (i.e., when it is invisible) and relate it to the phases of the moon.*
Awareness of the "energies" of the Sun and the Moon will eliminate the juxtaposition between light and darkness, true and false, high and low.
Even temples will become obsolete.

*The composition of this card uses the very deep timbres of the magnetic tape interspersed with the chords of The Emperor and alternating with the melody of The Magician and the beat note of The Hermit.*
*The music in these cards is influenced by the need to assign the Sun a masculine nature in contrast with the Moon.*
*A deeper chord than the others will lead us into the Sun itself: we will be surrounded by its warmth and energy, we will loose our fear and realise we are living in a different and exciting dimension.*
*We emanate and are emanated.*
*The piece ends with four solemn chord sounds symbolising the completed and perfect merger between masculine and feminine polarities of the body, soul and spirit.*

# the Moon

The Moon is considered the mother of fertility and symbol of the concept of procreation.
At night she exploits her occult relationship with liquids and draws inside her the generating seed that the Sun generously scatters on Earth through its rays and warmth.

*The trials and tribulations of our life on earth are there to "teach" us: when we pass these tests we will be compensated with final initiation.*
We should act so that the true light of The Moon can embrace us with her paleness and beauty, only then will we find the lost word and reforge the broken key.

*To achieve full understanding of this crucial Trump, The Magician will have to carefully study the phases of the moon above all during the day (i.e., when it is invisible) and relate it to the sun's activity.*
Understanding The Moon and The Sun means reaching the final rung of the esoteric ladder where high and low, true and false, darkness and light no longer exist.
Even temples will become obsolete.

The composition of this card is exemplified by the metallic timbres of the magnetic tape interspersed with the melismata of The High Priestess and alternating with the notes of the tune of The Magician. The piece ends with sounds that recall the rhythmic, "unique" impulses in the finale of The Empress, sounds which are now fully aware because they have finally become "chords". With the tunes of The High Priestess and The Empress the music is influenced by the need to give the Moon a feminine nature contrasting the masculine nature of the Sun.

A deeper chord than the others will lead us into the Moon itself: we will be surrounded by its paleness and beauty, we will loose our fear and realise we are living in a different and exciting dimension.

*We emanate and are emanated.*

The piece ends with four solemn chord sounds symbolising the completed and perfect merger between feminine and masculine polarities of the body, soul and spirit.

# Judgement

The spirit of The Magician, having reached the highest level of his *Initiation*, has been able to assimilate the "thoughts" that slept in the depths of the Sun and Moon.
I ask myself whether he hasn't become an Angel who by blowing his trumpet is able to simultaneously communicate with all the different levels of awareness.
I don't know… what I do know is that now Man is able to "understand" and penetrate the wonderful works of Nature and Art; he's able to understand its true beauty and reveal their secrets.
The card makes it possible to understand and become aware of the Great Task iconographically symbolised by three human figures who are none other than the Father (The Sun), the Mother (The Moon) and the Son born from their new union.
Even in this dimension we once again find the miracle of the number THREE.

*The composition is a "fugato" in which the tune is the same as The Magician but performed with "augmented" and "diminished" rhythmic values (i.e., with notes that are longer or shorter than the original ones) and a faster more diversified tempo (3/4 in The Magician and 4/4 in the Judgement).*

*For the first time we realise three Guitars are performing: the electric guitar to which we had assigned the role associated with instinctivity and representing the feminine (the Moon); the Baroque guitar representing the masculine (the Sun); the "New Man", portrayed by a classical guitar.*

*I wanted to end with a piece that somehow recalled what I believe represents the highest and most perfect form ever created by the human mind in the world of music: the Fugue.*

*Part VII* **card n. 22**

# the World

What's happening? I feel as if I'm in a whirlwind that at supersonic speed is taking me back, or perhaps forward… I don't know where I'm going… I think I see strange people – a old tramp-hermit holding an electric torch, a king who looks like my father, an empress who looks like my mother, two lovers who are in fact my daughter and her fiancée. I shiver when I see a devil who looks like my chartered accountant. And this deafening noise is not that of a royal Chariot, but the bus going "past my house"!!! Like an animated puzzle I watch as the thousand shards of the broken mirror visualised at the beginning of my journey quickly reassemble and reflect the image of just one me. What a strange feeling: did I dream or did I really experience all this?

*And yet I'm still surrounded by the strange echoes I heard when I concentrated on The Magician.*
*I start to play my guitar again trying to follow the sounds that still linger in my head – the High Priestess, the Empress, the Emperor and the Pope. In turn they harmonically come closer to the notes of my "song", but slowly vanish.*

*So, now I'm truly alone and I'm able to listen to this song of mine, so physical and melancholy; but however much I try it doesn't ever really end, so it remains hanging in the air…*

# The Magician
by Bruno Battisti D'Amario

# Tarot cards
## meditation and music

| track | title | | length |
|---|---|---|---|
| Track n° 1 | I | The Magician | 2'01" |
| Track n° 2 | II | The High Priestess | 2'23" |
| Track n° 3 | III | The Empress | 2'29" |
| Track n° 4 | IV | The Emperor | 2'55" |
| Track n° 5 | V | The Pope | 2'11" |
| Track n° 6 | VI | The Lovers | 3'41" |
| Track n° 7 | IX | The Hermit | 2'31" |
| Track n° 8 | VII | The Chariot | 3'08" |
| Track n° 9 | VIII | Justice | 3'18" |
| Track n° 10 | XV | The Devil | 2'35" |
| Track n° 11 | XIII | Death | 2'07" |
| Track n° 12 | XI | Strength | 2'11" |
| Track n° 13 | XVI | The Tower | 3'05" |
| Track n° 14 | XIV | Temperance | 3'19" |
| Track n° 15 | X | The Wheel of Fortune | 2'35" |
| Track n° 16 | 0 | The Fool | 3'50" |
| Track n° 17 | XVII | The Stars | 2'40" |
| Track n° 18 | XII | The Hanged Man | 2'22" |
| Track n° 19 | XIX | The Sun | 3'34" |
| Track n° 20 | XVIII | The Moon | 3'23" |
| Track n° 21 | XX | Judgement | 3'10" |
| Track n° 22 | XXI | The World | 4'42" |

*Guitarist Bruno Battisti D'Amario (guitar Ignacio Fleta)*
*The magnetic tape was recorded in the studios of Edipan-records*
*Viale Mazzini 6 – Rome*

Finito di stampare nel mese di aprile 2011
**GANGEMI EDITORE** SPA –
www.gangemieditore.it